GUS and GRANDPA
Go Fishing

Claudia Mills ★ Pictures by Catherine Stock

Farrar, Straus and Giroux

New York

*In memory of my father, who loved to go bass
fishing in New Hampshire*
—C.M.

*In memory of my dad, who took me trout
fishing in Colorado*
—C.S.

Text copyright © 2003 by Claudia Mills
Illustrations copyright © 2003 by Catherine Stock
All rights reserved
Distributed in Canada by Douglas & McIntyre Ltd.
Color separations by Phoenix Color Corporation
Printed and bound in the United States of America by Phoenix Color Corporation
First edition, 2003
1 3 5 7 9 10 8 6 4 2

Library of Congress Cataloging-in-Publication Data
Mills, Claudia.
    Gus and Grandpa go fishing / Claudia Mills ; pictures by Catherine Stock.— 1st ed.
    p. cm.
    Summary: Gus goes fishing for the first time and receives expert guidance from
his grandfather.
    ISBN 0-374-32815-3
    [1. Fishing—Fiction. 2. Grandfathers—Fiction.] I. Stock, Catherine, ill. II. Title.

PZ7.M63963 Guef 2002
[E]—dc21

                                                                    2002022396

Casting

Grandpa knew a secret lake.
To get there,
Mommy had to drive up
a long, winding dirt road.
The road was bumpy.
It made Gus's stomach
feel bumpy, too.

When they reached the lake,
Gus threw sticks for Skipper.

Grandpa had two old
fishing poles.
He gave one to Gus.
Gus's father had a brand-new rod.
Daddy liked to order things
from catalogs.
But he never got around
to using them.

Gus's mother didn't have
a fishing pole.
"I don't like fishing,"
she said.
"I just like having a picnic
by a beautiful lake."

Grandpa put a lure
on the end of Gus's line.
Then he showed Gus
how to cast.
Grandpa's line sailed out
over the lake
in a perfect arc.

When Gus swung his pole,
his line got all tangled.
If he didn't learn
to cast better,
he'd end up catching Skipper
instead of a fish.

Gus tried again.
The line got twisted
around his shoes.
It was tighter than ten shoelaces
tied by Gus's mother.
Grandpa had to cut it off
with his knife.

"Maybe you should cast for him,"
Gus's father said.

"He can do it,"
Grandpa said.

Gus flicked his wrist again.
Nothing happened.
He tried once more.
This time his line soared
in a perfect arc,
just like Grandpa's.

Gus didn't wait for a fish to bite.
He reeled his line in
as fast as he could,
and cast again,
and again,
and again.
He didn't care
if he ever caught a fish.
Casting was enough.

The Tug on the Line

Half an hour later,
Gus decided
that he *did* care
if he ever caught a fish.
He wound his line in slowly,
to give the fish a chance
to bite.

He jiggled the line
a little bit
so the fish would be sure
to see it.
He tried casting
from a rock
out in the water.

He tried casting
from an old log.
Nothing happened.
Nothing at all.

Then Grandpa caught a fish!
Gus and Daddy cheered.
Skipper barked.
Over by the picnic table,
Mommy waved
the tablecloth
like a flag.

Grandpa put the fish
in his creel
to take home with him.

"I want to catch a fish,"
Gus told Grandpa.

"Keep trying," Grandpa said.
"We know they're out there."

Daddy hadn't caught a fish
yet, either.
He was still trying to figure out
all the fancy features
of his new fishing rod.

Gus cast again.

His line lay on the water
like a long piece of string.

He was getting bored.

The fish must be
getting bored, too.

Now Gus didn't even bother
to wiggle his line.

Suddenly the line jerked.
Gus felt it tug.
"I have a fish!" he shouted.

"Reel it in," Grandpa said.
"Slowly . . . slowly."

The fish pulled hard.
Gus pulled harder.

Then Gus didn't feel the fish
pulling anymore.
"He got away,"
Gus said in a small voice.
He couldn't believe
his one and only fish was gone.
The lure was gone, too.

"Too bad," Daddy said.
Grandpa patted his shoulder.
Skipper licked his hand.

"Picnic time!" Mommy called.

The Family Fishermen

The picnic was good.
But it would have tasted better
if Gus's fish hadn't gotten away.
"At least you learned how to cast,"
Gus's mother said.
"I tried fishing once,
but I couldn't even
cast my line."

Gus didn't care about casting now.
Casting wasn't the point
of fishing.
Catching was.

After lunch,
Gus kept on trying
to catch a fish.
He stood in the same spot
where he had stood before.

He let the line
lie on the water
in the same way.
Then he started to reel it in.

The line jerked again!
"Grandpa!" Gus whispered.
He didn't want to shout
in case he scared the fish away.

"Steady," Grandpa said softly.
"You have him.
Steady."

Gus kept on reeling the line in.
There was his fish!
A big one!
Flopping on the end of his line!

Grandpa helped Gus scoop
the fish into the net.
Grandpa helped Gus take the fish
off the hook.
"Go show Mommy," he said.

Gus's mother was busy
packing up the picnic.
"Look!" Gus shouted.
He held up the squirming,
wiggling, jiggling fish
right next to her face
so she could see.
She turned around and screamed!

Gus and Grandpa and Daddy
started laughing.
Then Mommy laughed, too.
"I told you I didn't like fishing!"
she said.

Gus smiled at her.
He liked fishing.
His mother could tie shoelaces
better than Gus could tie them.
But she couldn't catch a fish
the way Gus could.

Gus's father hadn't caught
a fish, either.
He had given up
on his new fishing rod.

"I guess we're the fishermen
in this family,"
Grandpa said to Gus.

"I guess so, too," Gus said.

Gus's parents took Skipper
and went for a walk
through the woods.

Grandpa put a new lure
on Gus's line.
And the family fishermen
headed back to the lake
together.